T5-ADA-510

COLLEGE SPORTS TODAY

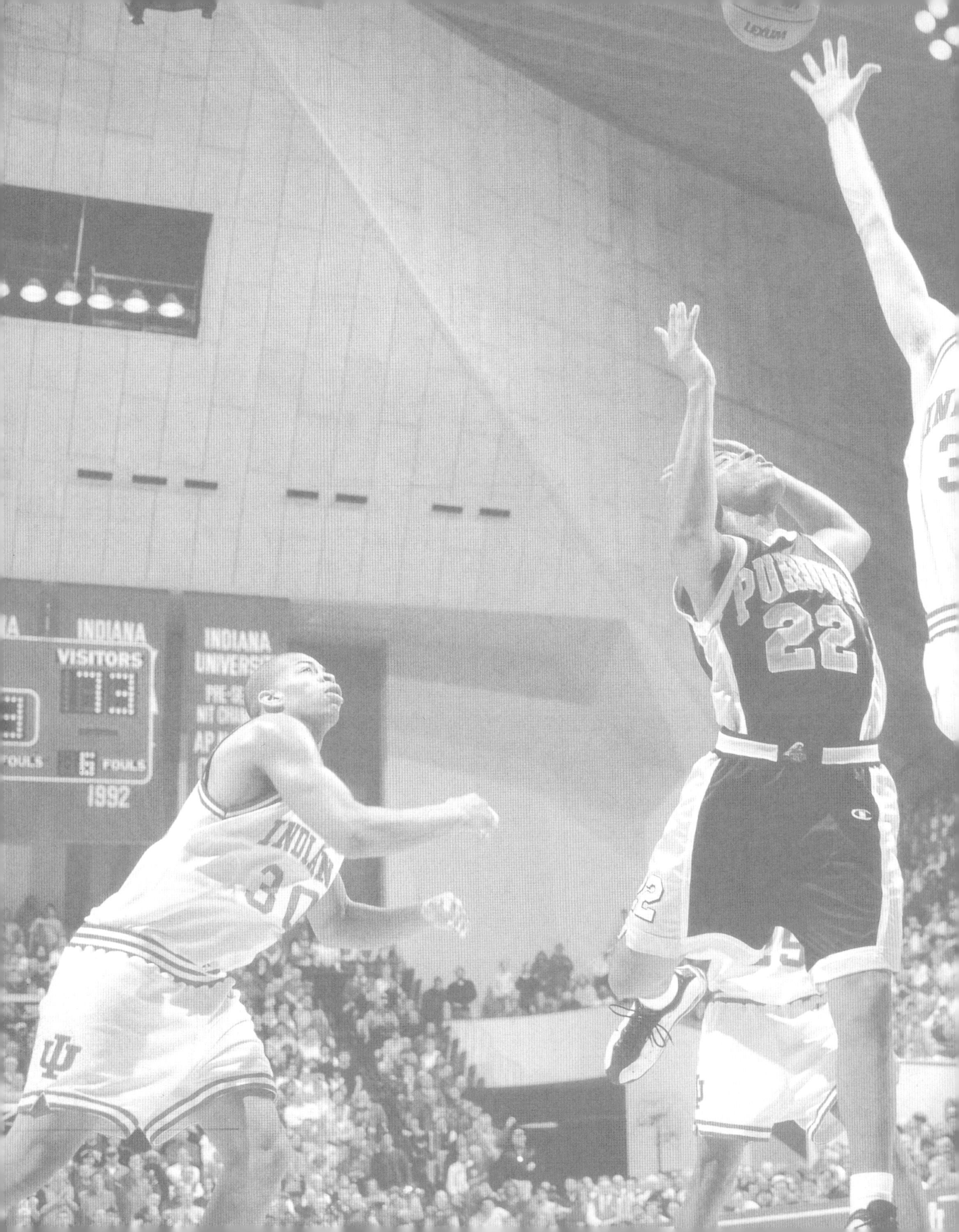
INDIANA
VISITORS
INDIANA
6 FOULS
FOULS
1992
22
INDIANA
30

COLLEGE SPORTS TODAY

HAIL HOOSIERS!
THE INDIANA HOOSIERS STORY
SUE VANDER HOOK

CREATIVE EDUCATION

Published by Creative Education
123 South Broad Street, Mankato, Minnesota 56001
Creative Education is an imprint of The Creative Company

Designed by Stephanie Blumenthal
Production design by The Design Lab
Editorial assistance by John Nichols

Photos by: Allsport USA, AP/Wide World Photos,
SportsChrome, and UPI/Corbis-Bettmann

Copyright © 2000 Creative Education.
International copyrights reserved in all countries.
No part of this book may be reproduced in any form
without written permission from the publisher.
Printed in the United States of America.

Library of Congress Cataloging-in-Publication Data

Vander Hook, Sue, 1949–
Hail Hoosiers! the Indiana Hoosiers story / by Sue Vander Hook.
p. cm. — (College basketball today)
Summary: Examines the history of the Indiana University basketball program.
ISBN: 0-88682-990-9

1. Indiana University, Bloomington—Basketball—History—Juvenile literature. 2. Indiana Hoosiers (Basketball team)—History—Juvenile literature. [1. Indiana Hoosiers (Basketball team)—History. 2. Basketball—History.] I. Title. II. Series: College basketball today (Mankato, Minn.)

GV885.43.I53V36   1999
796.323'63'09772255—dc21   98-30935

First Edition

2 4 6 8 9 7 5 3 1

As the last few seconds of the game tick off the clock, a roar of approval builds in Assembly Hall. No matter how the victory comes, whether by a last-second three-pointer that spins endlessly on the rim before dropping or by a 30-point blowout, the Indiana fans cheer thunderously for their Hoosiers. Should the team lose in an upset, the Assembly Hall faithful still boisterously show their support. This is called "Hoosier Hysteria." Fans in Bloomington, Indiana, know that they are cheering for a roster of fine young men that has included such names as Isiah Thomas, Steve Alford, and Calbert Cheaney over the years. These are the Indiana Hoosiers, admired by fans and respected by foes for their hard-nosed, tireless style of play—a style that has brought multiple national championships home to Indiana.

INDIANA'S

CHAMPIONSHIP

BANNERS EARNED

UNDER KNIGHT

SMALL TOWN BEGINNINGS

Hoosier Hysteria centers on the small college city of Bloomington, Indiana. With 60,000 residents, Bloomington sits nestled amidst the corn and soybean fields of the Midwest. Immortalized in the song "Small Town," the city is home to rock star John Mellencamp. But more importantly to basketball fans, Bloomington is home to Indiana University.

Indiana University is a well-respected school founded in 1820 that attracts 36,000 students each year, making it one of the nation's largest schools. Attending a big school in a small-town atmosphere gives students the best of both worlds, a unique trait of IU not lost on its students. "Bloomington is a place where a farm kid can begin to understand city life, and a city kid can learn to appreciate the sky," said former Hoosiers star and Chicago native Isiah Thomas. "I cherish the time I spent at Indiana."

The sport of basketball has been a part of Indiana University since 1901. The school's first team wasn't very good, going just 1–4 in its first season. But the fast-paced, team-oriented game was an instant hit in Indiana, and it did not take long for the sport to put down roots in the state's fertile soil. "You can travel anywhere in Indiana, from the steel mills of Gary to the wheat

FANS OF ALL AGES ADMIRE THEIR BELOVED HOOSIERS; COACH BOBBY KNIGHT (BELOW)

JARROD ODLE

fields of any small town, and no matter where you look, there is a basketball hoop with at least one kid shooting at it," said former IU star Damon Bailey. "It's not a sport in this state—it's more like a religion."

Despite the poor record of the school's first team, interest quickly grew in the new sport. In 1902, 50 players tried out for the squad, and the team improved to a 4–4 mark. The program continued upward from there. In 1921, Everett Dean became Indiana's first basketball All-American. Three years later, Dean began a Hoosiers tradition by returning as head coach. It was that year, in 1924, that Indiana played its first game against Kentucky, winning 20–18 and beginning a rivalry between the neighboring states that continues to this day.

THE FIRST CHAMPIONSHIP

When Dean stepped down as Hoosiers coach, the next man to fill the role was Emmett "Branch" McCracken, another Indiana alumnus who had earned All-American honors in 1930. In 1939, his first year at the helm of the Hoosiers, McCracken led his "Merry Macs" to a 17–3 record. The next year would be even better.

Purdue had won the Big Ten crown in 1940 with a 16–4 record, but its coach, Ward "Piggy" Lambert, thought that playing 20 games in a season was enough. He turned down the National Collegiate Athletic Association's (NCAA) post-season tournament invitation

ALL-BIG TEN FORWARD

QUINN BUCKNER (ABOVE);

COACH "BRANCH"

MCCRACKEN (BELOW)

and suggested that Indiana—a team that had beaten his twice during the year—be invited instead. The Hoosiers gladly accepted the chance to continue playing.

In the tournament's first round, Indiana's fast-break offense, led by speedsters Marv Huffman and Jay McCreary, baffled Springfield College and came away with a 48–24 win. The Hoosiers then beat Duquesne 39–30 before knocking off Kansas 60–42 to claim their first NCAA championship—not bad considering that Indiana should not have even been in the tournament.

Indiana's rise as a basketball powerhouse was temporarily interrupted by World War II. When Coach McCracken joined the war effort in 1943, the Hoosiers' record took a nosedive. On his return on December 2, 1946, a record crowd of 7,631 crammed into the Hoosier Fieldhouse to watch "Big Mac" and his Merry Macs destroy Wabash 69–46. McCracken, known as a workaholic who reportedly was fueled by 30 cups of coffee per day, coached until 1965 and ended his career with 364 victories.

In the late 1940s and early '50s, the Hoosiers continued to win behind the efforts of All-Americans John Wallace, Lou Watson, and Bill Garrett. But it wasn't until 1953 that Indiana captured its first undisputed Big Ten title. That season, the Hoosiers went 17–1 in the conference (their lone loss came in a hard-fought game against Minnesota in Minneapolis) under the leadership of All-American sophomore Don Schlundt.

DOMINATING CENTER DON SCHLUNDT (ABOVE); 1972–73 BIG TEN MVP STEVE DOWNING (LEFT, #32)

HIGH-SCORING GUARD STEVE ALFORD

Although freshmen in that era normally sat out a year while adjusting to college life, Schlundt was allowed to play his freshman year due to the shortage of players caused by the Korean War. Schlundt, who stood 6-foot-10 but had the agility of a quick guard, dominated games as a sophomore and led the Big Ten in scoring.

With his 25 points-per-game scoring average, Schlundt took the Hoosiers to the 1953 NCAA title game against the Kansas Jayhawks in Kansas City. With a home crowd cheering on the Jayhawks, the game came down to a pair of free throws with 12 seconds remaining. Hoosiers guard Bob "Slick" Leonard stood nervously at the line while 9,000 fans screamed for him to miss. He did.

Kansas coach Phog Allen, a legend in college coaching circles, called a timeout to let Leonard think about his second free throw. "I was scared to death," Leonard recalled. Despite his anxiety, Leonard sank the second shot to silence the crowd and give Indiana its second NCAA crown, 69–68.

Schlundt went on to become a three-time All-American, finishing his career as college basketball's Player of the Year in 1955. Following graduation, he turned down a $5,500 offer to play for the Syracuse Nationals of the National Basketball Association and became an insurance salesman instead.

COACH BOBBY KNIGHT

(ABOVE); ANDRAE

PATTERSON (BELOW)

PLAYER PORTRAIT

NAME: Don Schlundt
DIED: October 10, 1985
HEIGHT/WEIGHT: 6-foot-10/235 pounds
POSITION: Center
SEASONS PLAYED: 1951-52–1954-55
AWARDS/HONORS: All-Big Ten selection (1952-53, 1953-54, 1954-55), All-American (1952-53, 1953-54, 1954-55), Big Ten MVP (1952-53)

Schlundt dominated the Big Ten Conference in the early 1950s, leading the Hoosiers in scoring in each of his four seasons and in rebounding three years. With his astounding natural ability and great size, Schlundt was virtually unstoppable when he got the ball. His career points-per-game average of 23.3 tops the Hoosiers' all-time list.

STATISTICS:

Season	Points per game	Rebounds per game
1951–52	17.1	7.2
1952–53	25.4	8.5
1953–54	24.3	11.1
1954–55	26.0	9.8

PLAYER PORTRAIT

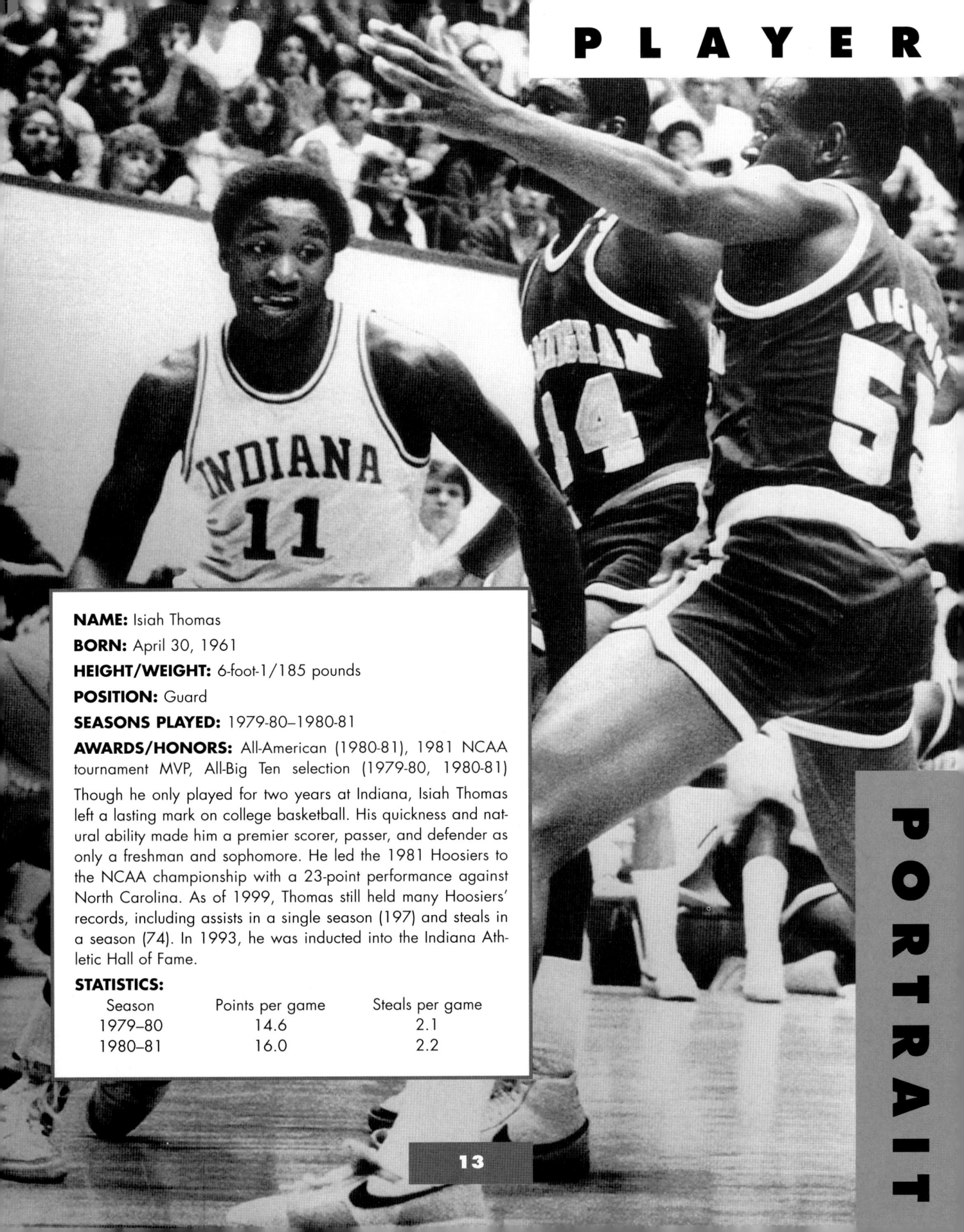

NAME: Isiah Thomas
BORN: April 30, 1961
HEIGHT/WEIGHT: 6-foot-1/185 pounds
POSITION: Guard
SEASONS PLAYED: 1979-80–1980-81
AWARDS/HONORS: All-American (1980-81), 1981 NCAA tournament MVP, All-Big Ten selection (1979-80, 1980-81)

Though he only played for two years at Indiana, Isiah Thomas left a lasting mark on college basketball. His quickness and natural ability made him a premier scorer, passer, and defender as only a freshman and sophomore. He led the 1981 Hoosiers to the NCAA championship with a 23-point performance against North Carolina. As of 1999, Thomas still held many Hoosiers' records, including assists in a single season (197) and steals in a season (74). In 1993, he was inducted into the Indiana Athletic Hall of Fame.

STATISTICS:

Season	Points per game	Steals per game
1979–80	14.6	2.1
1980–81	16.0	2.2

BOBBY KNIGHT: CONTROVERSIAL SUCCESS

After the 1953 national title, Indiana basketball continued to prosper, but the team could not get back to the championship for the remainder of the 1950s and '60s. Then, in 1971, the Hoosiers program was placed in the hands of a 31-year-old coaching prodigy by the name of Bobby Knight.

Prior to coming to Indiana, Knight had turned heads in the basketball world by transforming undersized and underskilled Army teams into consistent winners. Although the academy at West Point required all incoming cadets to be 6-foot-6 or shorter (for military reasons), Knight's squads won 20 games three times during his six seasons as Army coach.

Since his arrival at Indiana, there has not been a more successful—or controversial—coach than Bobby Knight. In nearly 30 years at Indiana, Knight has led the Hoosiers to several national championships, numerous Big Ten titles, and an NCAA tournament berth practically every season. The fiery leader became the youngest coach to ever reach 700 career wins, and by 1998 he ranked second among active coaches in number of wins.

INDIANA SHARP-SHOOTERS GREG GRAHAM (ABOVE) AND STEVE ALFORD (BELOW)

FORWARD LARRY RICHARDSON

Knight is revered in Indiana. Biographer Paul Challen writes that "because of the statewide passion [for basketball], the head coach of the Indiana University basketball team has been elevated to near-God status, among young and old fans alike."

Knight is perhaps best known for his willingness to speak his mind. Nicknamed "The General" by sports commentator Dick Vitale for his tough style of leadership, Knight has earned a reputation for being a bit prickly toward both players and the media. Players learn this quickly. As Challen writes, "If you play ball at Indiana University, you play it the way coach Knight wants you to play, or you get out of Bloomington."

Knight is extremely loyal to his players, however. When Indiana center Landon Turner suffered a paralyzing spinal injury in a car accident after his junior year in 1981, Knight created a trust fund to help pay his medical expenses. Turner's parents praised Knight: "Once you become a part of the Indiana basketball family, you always remain a part of it. Coach Knight is very loyal to not only the players in the current program, but to past players and their families as well."

Some players, however, have been openly critical of Coach Knight. They complain that his coaching methods, which often include screaming, yelling, and berating players, are abusive. One

FORWARD SCOTT MAY (ABOVE); LUKE RECKER AND ROB TURNER (BELOW)

such player is former Hoosiers guard Neil Reed. After Indiana was trounced by Colorado 80–62 in the first round of the 1997 NCAA tournament, Knight met with his three junior players—Reed, center Richard Mandeville, and forward Andrae Patterson—and suggested that they all transfer to another school. Knight said they would receive little playing time their senior year and might be happier elsewhere.

Patterson and Mandeville stayed at Indiana, but Reed left on bitter terms. He spoke openly to the press about "verbal attacks and physical assaults," but many of Knight's former and then-current players rushed to his defense. "Coach Knight is intense about what he does, and sometimes people misinterpret that," said Alan Henderson, a former Hoosiers forward and current NBA player. "He's intense about the game."

Indiana boosters point to the number of former assistant coaches and players who now coach other basketball teams as proof that Knight is on the right track. His most famous assistant, Mike Krzyzewski, has turned Duke into a perennial powerhouse. Others

1976 NATIONAL CHAMPIONSHIP (ABOVE); GUARD A.J. GUYTON (BELOW)

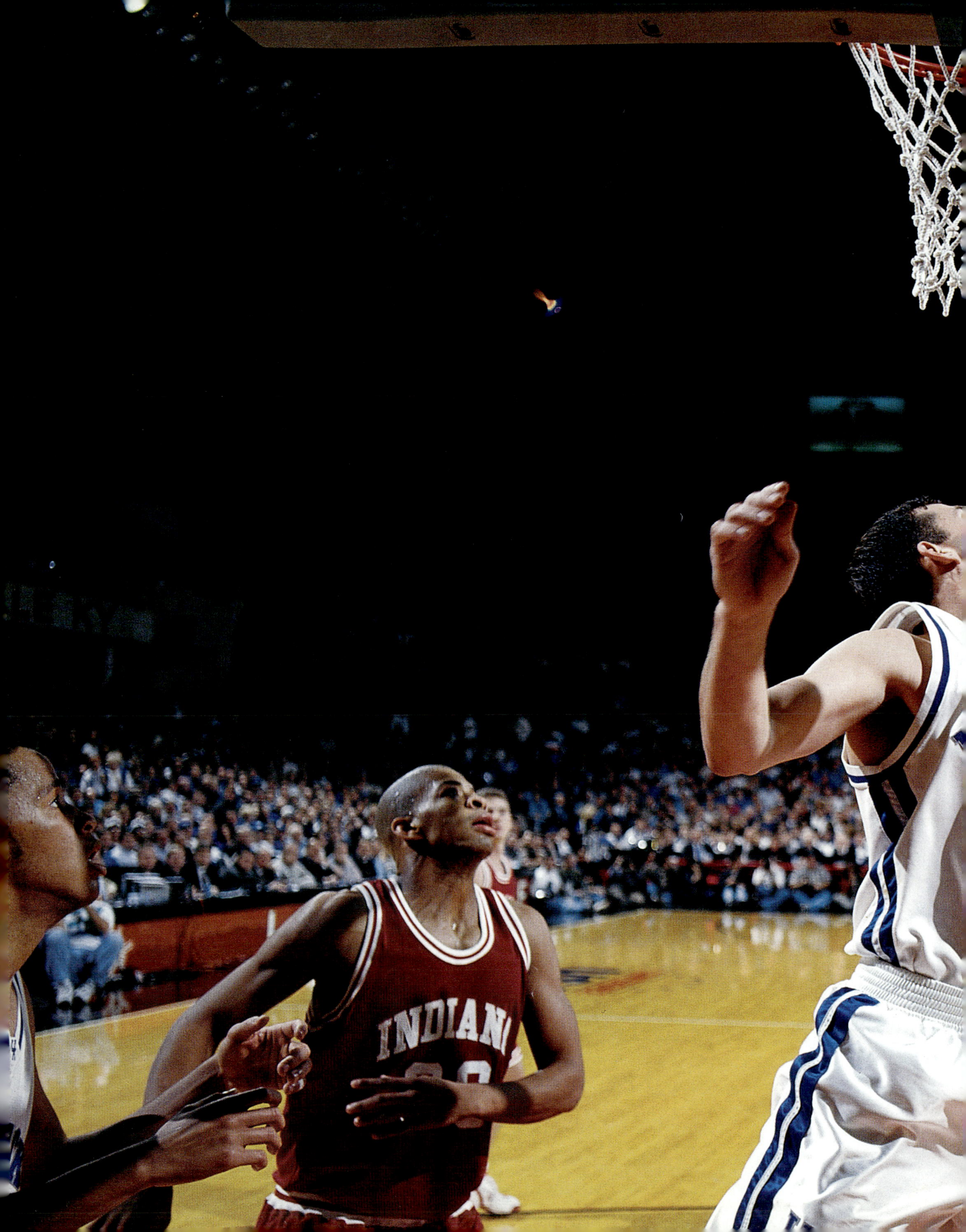
INDIANA

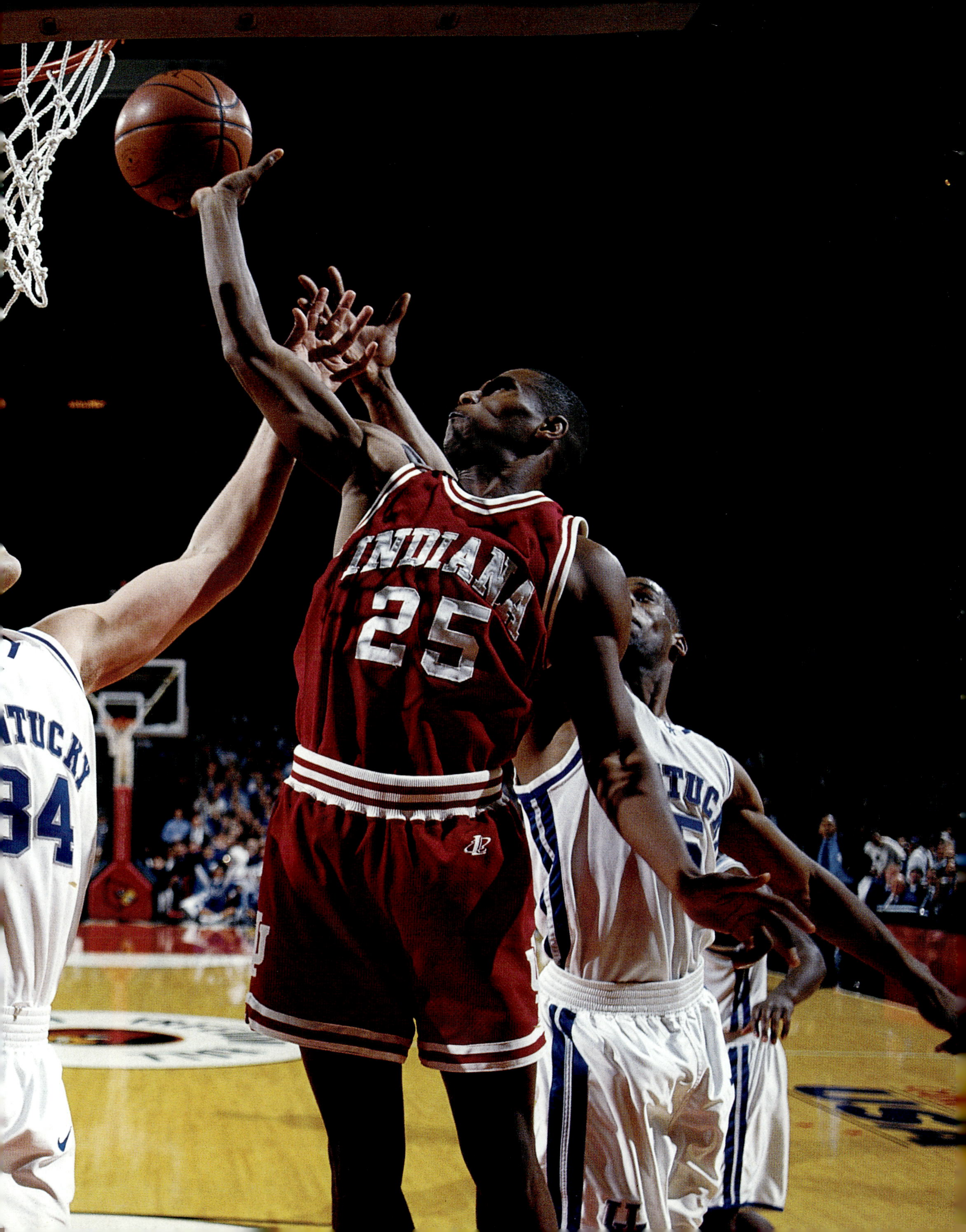
INDIANA
25
34

include long-time assistant Dan Dakich, who now coaches Bowling Green; former star guard Steve Alford, who heads the Iowa program; and Knight's own son, Pat, who coaches in the Continental Basketball Association (CBA).

"Coach Knight is not an easy man to please," said former Hoosiers player and NBA star Quinn Buckner. "He demands that you push yourself. If you're good, he wants you to be great. If you're great, he wants you to be awesome. Some people don't like to be pushed, but Coach Knight will confront you and make you come face to face with your potential."

INDIANA PERFECTION

Bobby Knight's record over three decades has proven that even teams short on talent can find consistent success with gutsy play and a never-say-die attitude.

In 1974–75, the Hoosiers lacked neither talent nor determination, and they posted a spotless 29–0 regular-season record and cruised to another Big Ten title. With the NCAA tournament about to begin, Indiana stood poised to dethrone UCLA as the nation's number-one team. But then fate dealt the Hoosiers a terrible blow. All-American forward Scott May broke his arm late in the season, and the weakened Hoosiers fell to Kentucky 92–90 in the regional finals—just one game short of the Final Four.

SHOT-BLOCKER DEAN GARRETT (ABOVE); TOUGH GUARD ANTWAAN RANDLE EL (BELOW)

Coach Knight was heartbroken over the loss of what he considered his greatest team ever, but he immediately went to work on the next season.

The Hoosiers shined again in 1975–76. Many basketball fans consider that year's team one of the best in the history of college hoops. That season, Scott May, Quinn Buckner, Bobby Wilkerson, and Kent Benson led Indiana to its fourth straight Big Ten title and a national championship with a perfect 32–0 record. The NCAA final, played in Philadelphia's Spectrum arena to help celebrate America's 200th birthday, pitted the Hoosiers against conference rival Michigan.

In the early going, it appeared that bad fortune would once again befall the Hoosiers when guard Bobby Wilkerson was knocked out of the game with a concussion. The Wolverines quickly jumped out to a 10-point lead, but Indiana, behind Scott May's 26 points and eight rebounds, roared back to post an easy 86–68 victory and capture the school's third NCAA crown. No college team has finished with a perfect record since. "We were a close team, and it shook us when Bobby got hurt," recalled forward Quinn Buckner. "But we wanted that win and that championship so bad that I don't think anything could have stopped us that day."

ISIAH TAKES THE HOOSIERS TO THE TOP

The Hoosiers and Knight continued to have great success through the end of the 1970s. Powered by the efforts of such standout players as forward Mike Woodson, Indiana remained among the country's elite programs. But unfortunately for Hoosiers fans, Knight's squads could not reclaim the national championship.

BALL-HAWKING GUARD ISIAH THOMAS SET MANY SCHOOL RECORDS IN STEALS AND ASSISTS.

COACH

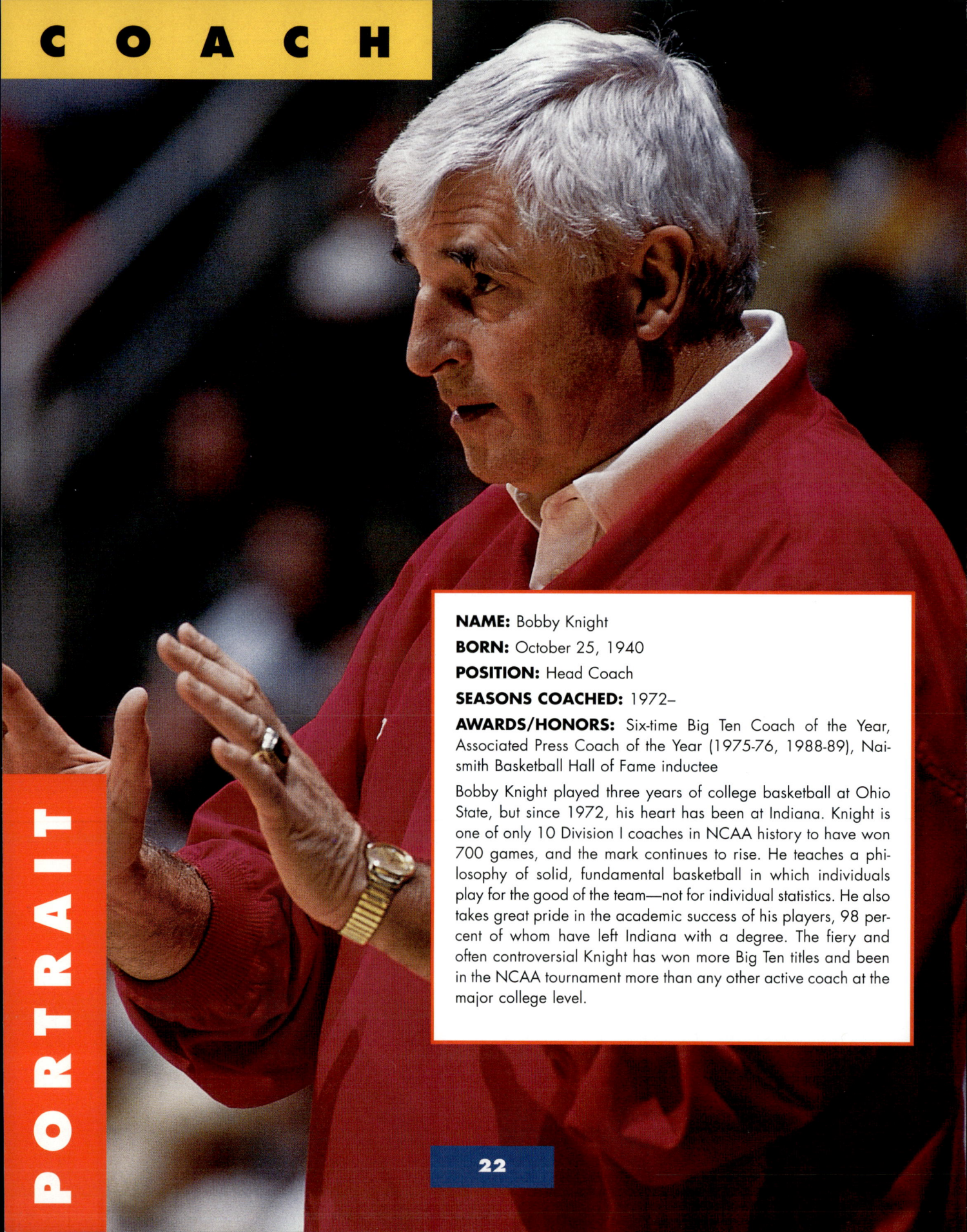

PORTRAIT

NAME: Bobby Knight
BORN: October 25, 1940
POSITION: Head Coach
SEASONS COACHED: 1972–
AWARDS/HONORS: Six-time Big Ten Coach of the Year, Associated Press Coach of the Year (1975-76, 1988-89), Naismith Basketball Hall of Fame inductee

Bobby Knight played three years of college basketball at Ohio State, but since 1972, his heart has been at Indiana. Knight is one of only 10 Division I coaches in NCAA history to have won 700 games, and the mark continues to rise. He teaches a philosophy of solid, fundamental basketball in which individuals play for the good of the team—not for individual statistics. He also takes great pride in the academic success of his players, 98 percent of whom have left Indiana with a degree. The fiery and often controversial Knight has won more Big Ten titles and been in the NCAA tournament more than any other active coach at the major college level.

PLAYER PORTRAIT

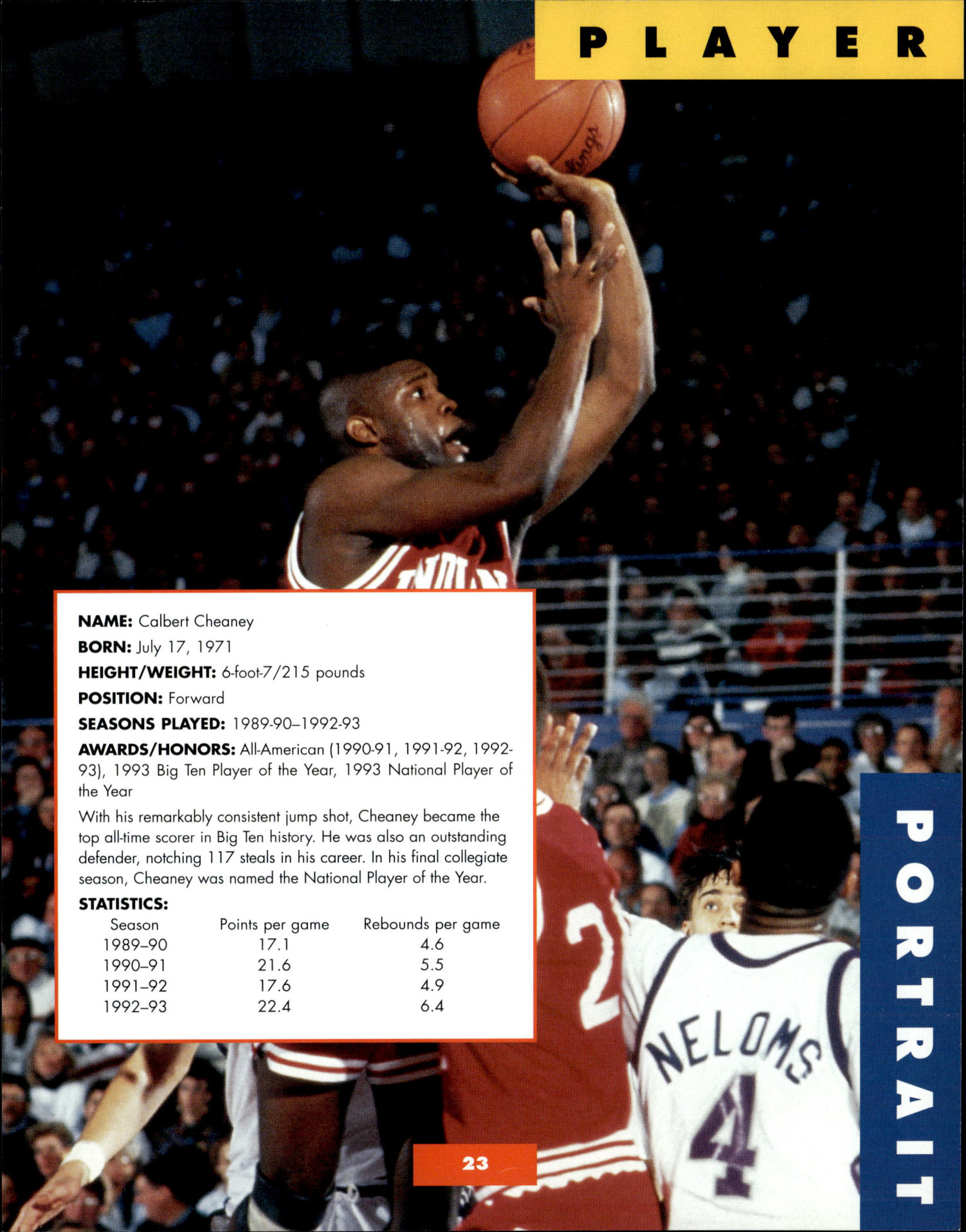

NAME: Calbert Cheaney

BORN: July 17, 1971

HEIGHT/WEIGHT: 6-foot-7/215 pounds

POSITION: Forward

SEASONS PLAYED: 1989-90–1992-93

AWARDS/HONORS: All-American (1990-91, 1991-92, 1992-93), 1993 Big Ten Player of the Year, 1993 National Player of the Year

With his remarkably consistent jump shot, Cheaney became the top all-time scorer in Big Ten history. He was also an outstanding defender, notching 117 steals in his career. In his final collegiate season, Cheaney was named the National Player of the Year.

STATISTICS:

Season	Points per game	Rebounds per game
1989–90	17.1	4.6
1990–91	21.6	5.5
1991–92	17.6	4.9
1992–93	22.4	6.4

HERO OF THE HOOSIERS'

1987 NATIONAL

CHAMPIONSHIP GAME,

KEITH SMART

Then, in 1979, a flashy point-guard sensation named Isiah Thomas arrived in Bloomington, and title expectations immediately rose. The 6-foot-1 Thomas possessed the easy smile of a child, but he also had the heart of a warrior and the on-court mentality of an assassin. During his freshman season, the charismatic floor leader led the Hoosiers in points, assists, steals, and free throw percentage. "He's a little stick of dynamite," Texas-El Paso head coach Don Haskins said after Thomas and the Hoosiers pasted his squad 75–43. "Bobby's got a good one there."

The 1979–80 Hoosiers captured the Big Ten title with a 13–5 conference mark, but Thomas's first season would end abruptly. A disappointing loss to conference foe Purdue knocked

Indiana from the NCAA tournament in the second round. "I hadn't lost too many big games before in my life," remembered Thomas. "I just expected that we would win the whole thing. That loss taught me a hard lesson."

The next season, a determined Thomas led Indiana to another Big Ten championship with a 14–4 record. The Hoosiers then marched through the early rounds of the NCAA tournament, dispatching teams with businesslike ease. Indiana's All-American point guard set the tone, but teammates Jim Thomas, Randy Wittman, and Ray Tolbert made Indiana unstoppable. "I felt that team really came together in the tournament," commented Knight. "Isiah was the focus, but when he learned to involve the other guys, we just took off."

In the NCAA finals, Indiana found themselves facing a familiar foe. Dean Smith's mighty North Carolina Tar Heels, featuring All-American forward James Worthy, lay in wait. In an earlier meeting that year, North Carolina had upended Indiana 65–56 in a game in which Thomas played so poorly that Coach Knight benched him.

The NCAA title game, however, would be a different story. Playing in front of 18,276 fans at the Philadelphia Spectrum, Indiana trailed North Carolina 27–26 at the half. "It was anybody's game right then," Thomas recalled. "But when I looked around at the guys' eyes in the locker room, I knew we were going to take it to them." The Hoosiers regrouped behind Isiah's 19-point second-half performance and pulled away to win 63–50. After leading the Hoosiers to their fourth

ANTWAAN RANDLE EL (ABOVE); OUTSTANDING '70S FORWARD STEVE GREEN (BELOW)

25

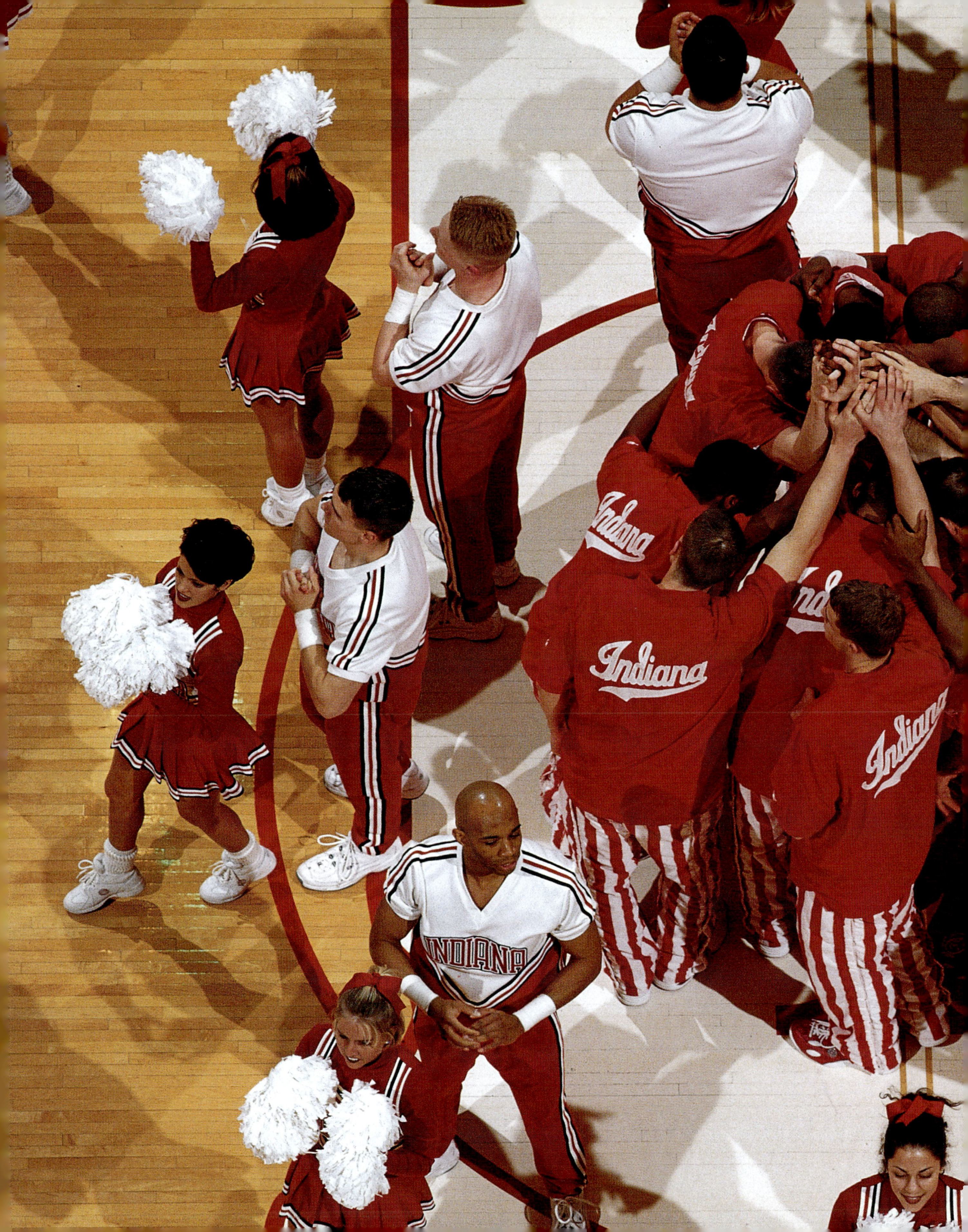
Indiana
Indiana
Indiana
INDIANA

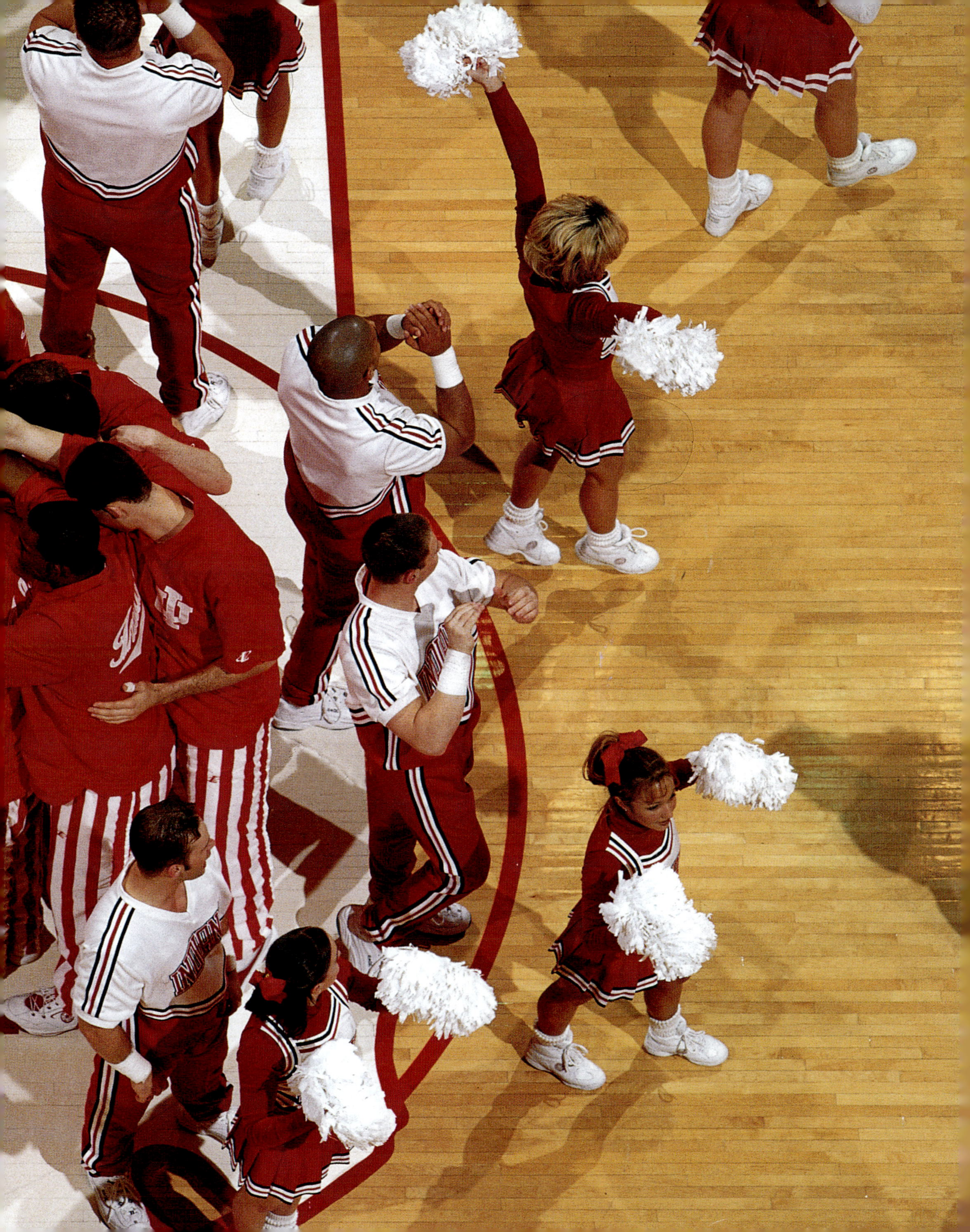

national championship and capturing the tournament MVP award, Thomas left IU to go on to greater fame with the NBA's Detroit Pistons. "Isiah was maybe the most talented kid I ever coached here at Indiana," Knight said. "Players like him come around only so often."

TITLE FIVE

The next time the Hoosiers found themselves challenging for a national championship, the leader of the team was not a phenomenally gifted athlete like Isiah Thomas. The driving force behind the 1986–87 Hoosiers was a slow, skinny, 6-foot-3 shooting guard by the name of Steve Alford. Alford was not naturally gifted, but he worked extremely hard on his game. "I knew I was never going to be a guy who could dominate games with athletic ability," explained the All-American. "My success came from a lot of hard work and using my head on the court."

Alford would run defenders ragged through screen after screen, eventually popping free long enough to unleash his deadly jump shot. "You don't have to be strong or fast to shoot well," said Alford, "you just have to work at it."

In his senior season, Alford averaged 22 points a game, powering Indiana to a 15–3 conference record and the 1987 Big

GUARD KEITH SMART (ABOVE); COACH KNIGHT LED INDIANA FOR THE 28TH SEASON IN 1998–99 (BELOW).

Ten title. During the NCAA tournament, the Hoosiers clubbed Fairfield, Auburn, and Duke aside before squeaking past Louisiana State 77–76 to reach the Final Four. In the semifinals, Indiana charged past the University of Nevada-Las Vegas 97–93 and came face to face with powerful Syracuse University.

The Orangemen were led by future NBA stars Rony Seikaly, Sherman Douglas, and Derrick Coleman, and many experts thought they would overwhelm the Hoosiers. But Alford knew better. "I knew if we played our game and didn't turn the ball over, we'd be tough to beat," he said.

In the title game, despite Alford's 23 points on 7-of-10 three-point shooting, Syracuse held a one-point lead as the second-half clock wound down. Indiana frantically worked the ball around, trying to free Alford for the game-winning shot. With only four seconds left, the ball ended up in the hands of junior guard Keith Smart, who calmly lofted a soft, 12-foot baseline jumper that swished through the net, putting Indiana up 74–73. The Orangemen stood in stunned disbelief as time expired.

Smart later admitted, "I just tossed it up. I didn't know where the ball went." Hoosiers fans, however, followed the arc of the ball and exploded in elation as Indiana captured its fifth national title. Smart, who went on to become a coach in the CBA, still

STEVE ALFORD (ABOVE) AND DEAN GARRETT (LEFT) WERE TWO HARD-WORKING HOOSIERS OF THE '80S.

cherished the moment years later. "To be a part of Indiana basketball history like that is something I will always treasure," he said.

KNIGHT'S PUPILS OF THE '90S

The 1990s have held a mixed bag of fortunes for Indiana basketball. In the early part of the decade, All-American forward Calbert Cheaney thrilled fans by scoring a school-record 2,613 points during his years at Bloomington. The 6-foot-7 sharpshooter was the driving force behind the Hoosiers' 1992 trip to the Final Four. But on the downside, beginning in 1994–95, Indiana suffered through four straight seasons of 10 losses or more. Although many schools would be more than happy with the Hoosiers' recent records, being simply good is not acceptable to Coach Knight and Indiana. "I've been somewhat disappointed in the last few seasons," Knight said, "but I think we can get back to playing the type of basketball people around here are used to seeing."

The type of basketball that former stars such as Quinn Buckner, Isiah Thomas, and Steve Alford played might be hard to duplicate, but the current crop of IU stars appears to be up to the task. Impact players such as guard A.J. Guyton and swingman Luke Recker have kept optimism in Bloomington at a consistent high.

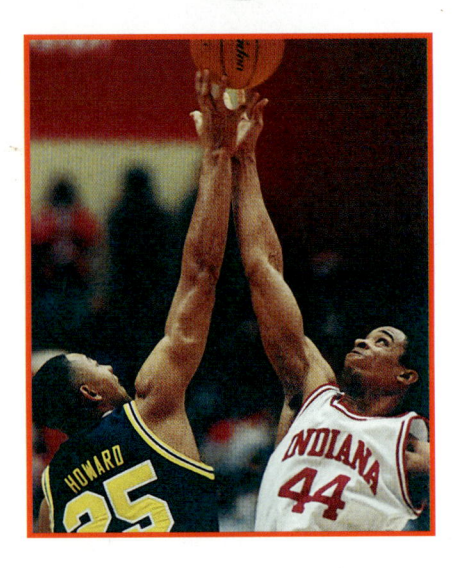

FORWARD ALAN HENDERSON (ABOVE) AND QUICK POINT GUARD MICHAEL LEWIS (BELOW)

EXPLOSIVE SHOOTING GUARD A.J. GUYTON

WITH THE EXPERIENCED COACH KNIGHT AT THE HELM, THE FUTURE OF HOOSIERS BASKETBALL IS BRIGHT.

The 6-foot-1 Guyton, whom many experts expected to go pro at the end of the 1998–99 season, earned first-team All-Big Ten honors in 1997–98 by torching opponents with 16.8 points per game. The speedy guard shot 44 percent from the three-point arc and chipped in 3.5 rebounds and 3.7 assists per game. The duty of distributing the ball to Guyton and other Hoosiers playmakers should fall to guard Michael Lewis, who has proven to be a solid point man.

Recker was a fiery, versatile ballplayer who epitomized Indiana's gritty style of play. The 6-foot-6, 200-pound swingman could move through screens effortlessly, shoot off the dribble, and take the ball to the hoop with authority. Although Recker's intensity sometimes turned into overaggression, Knight knew that he had the makings of an All-American. "Recker's a kid who makes things happen on the floor," Knight said. "He needs to work harder on defense, but he's a battler, and I like that."

The Hoosiers also looked to 6-foot-7, 230-pound forward Lynn Washington, a transfer from San Jose, California, Community College. "Washington will give us an element of strength and toughness we haven't had around here in great quantities the last few years," observed Knight. "I like his game." Guard Dane Fife is another Hoosiers player to watch in the future. "He's one tough kid who loves to compete," Knight said.

With Knight's strong roster ready to wreak havoc in the Big Ten Conference, fans at Assembly Hall will likely be witnessing more Indiana milestones in the seasons ahead. As one of basketball's greatest active coaches continues to drive Indiana basketball, a whole new wave of Hoosier Hysteria is ready to begin.